WHAT'S THE TIME, RORY WO

for Calum, Megan, Olwen, Brendan & Charlotte

What's the time, RORY WOLF?

Story and pictures by

GILLIAN McCLURE

André Deutsch Children's Books
Scholastic Children's Books
London

Scholastic Children's Books,
Scholastic Publications Ltd,
7-9 Pratt Street, London NW1 0AE, UK

Scholastic Inc.,
730 Broadway, New York, NY 10003, USA

Scholastic Canada Ltd,
123 Newkirk Road, Richmond Hill,
Ontario, Canada L4C 3G5

Ashton Scholastic Pty Ltd,
PO Box 579, Gosford, New South Wales,
Australia

Ashton Scholastic Ltd,
Private Bag 1, Penrose, Auckland,
New Zealand

First published by Andre Deutsch Children's Books, 1982

Copyright © 1982 by Gillian McClure

ISBN: 0 590 55607 X

Printed in Hong Kong

10 9 8 7 6 5

Gillian McClure has asserted her moral right to be identified
as the author of the work in accordance with the Copyright,
Design and Patents Act 1988.

High on a windy mountain in a forest that clung to a slope, lived a wolf called Rory. The forest had grown dismal and gloomy since Rory Wolf had made it his home.

At first it had been full of birds, animals and
flowers. But Rory Wolf had eaten them all. He had
gobbled up his enemies first and then when winters
were harsh and food scarce he had turned on his
friends and neighbours too.

Now there was nothing
left in the forest except
Rory Wolf, a very lonely
and hungry wolf.

A little way down the mountain was a village. Rory Wolf found a rubbish dump outside it and enough food to stay alive. But he wanted more than food, he wanted friends.

"Where can a wolf find a friend?" he howled.

Up the mountain he saw only cold stars shining on the wild windswept slopes, but down the mountain he saw the village and warm lamplight glowing in the windows.

"More life down there," he growled.

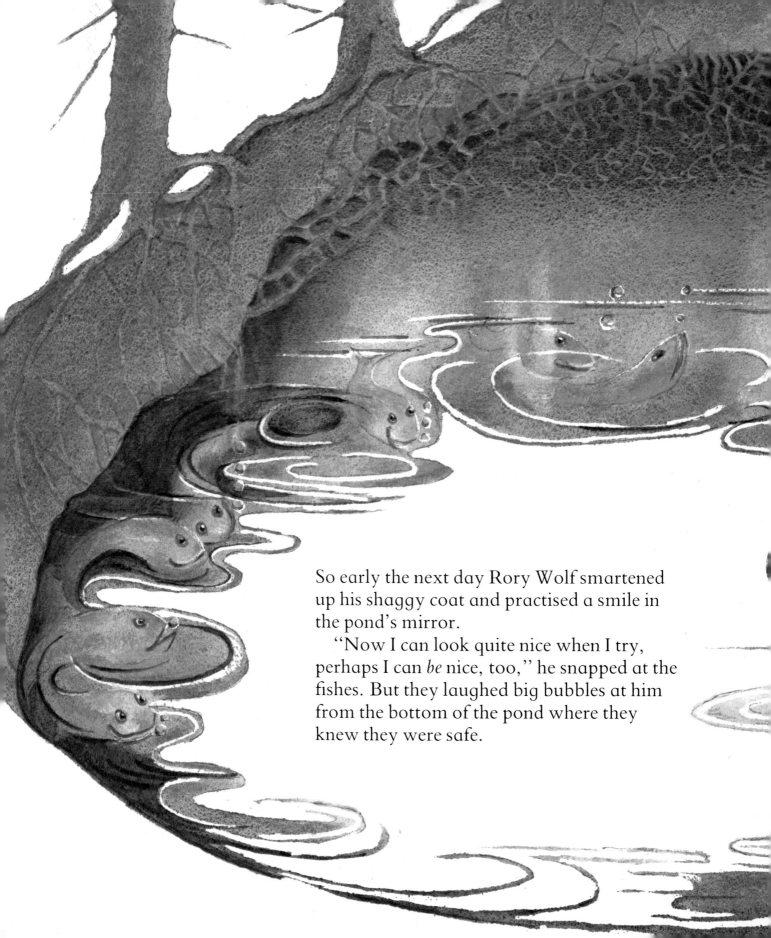

So early the next day Rory Wolf smartened up his shaggy coat and practised a smile in the pond's mirror.

"Now I can look quite nice when I try, perhaps I can *be* nice, too," he snapped at the fishes. But they laughed big bubbles at him from the bottom of the pond where they knew they were safe.

Rory Wolf set off down towards the village and on the way he met a little old woman. Rory Wolf liked little old women because they reminded him of Red Riding Hood's granny.

"Excuse me, my good old woman," Rory Wolf meant to say, but the cold air had made his voice gruff and growly.

"Ahhhhhhhhhhhhh!" gasped the old woman.

"Ugh Ugh Ugh!" coughed the wolf.

"Help!" cried the old woman.

"ARrrrrrrrrrrr!" wheezed the wolf.

"Wolf!" screamed the old woman. "Wolf wolf!" she screeched and ran down the road on her old creaking legs.

Rory Wolf was surprised and a little taken aback.

"What's wrong? I'm not a snappy wolf and I'm certainly not a snarly wolf."

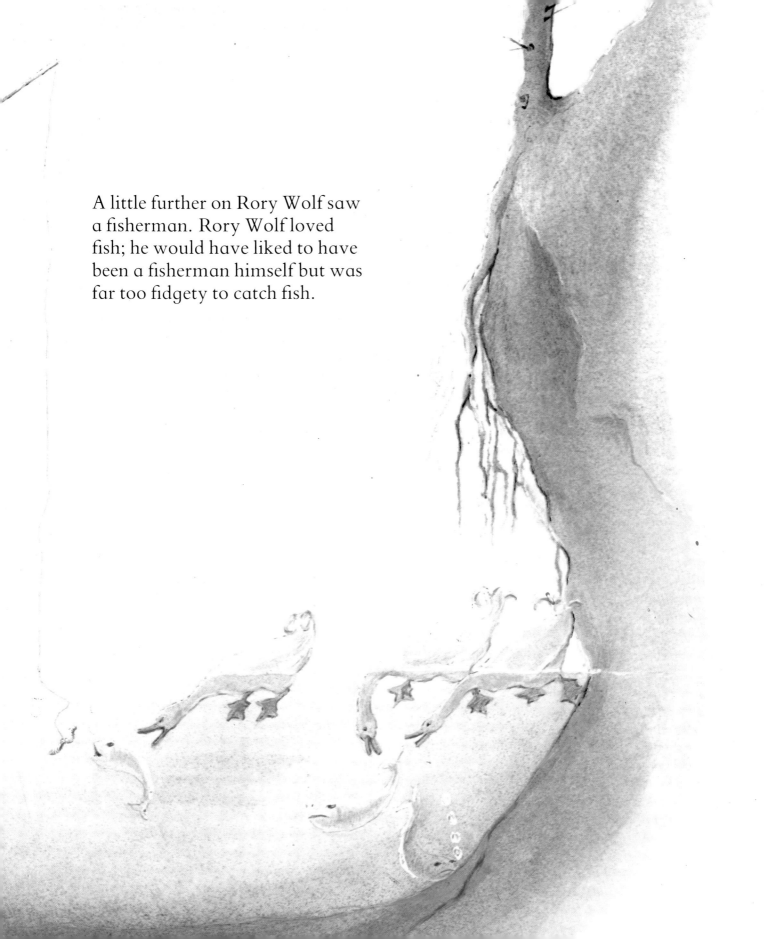

A little further on Rory Wolf saw a fisherman. Rory Wolf loved fish; he would have liked to have been a fisherman himself but was far too fidgety to catch fish.

"Any luck?" growled the wolf, his mouth watering.

"Ooooooh!" shouted the fisherman.

"Got a fish?" asked the wolf excitedly.

"Splash!" went the fisherman.

"Water cold?" growled the wolf, surprised.

"Ssssssssssssplutter!" went the fisherman, going under and surfacing again further downstream.

Rory Wolf was puzzled and a little hurt. "What's wrong? I'm not a wicked wolf and I'm certainly not a wilful wolf."

And Rory Wolf went on his way.

He reached the village and heard a band playing. Rory Wolf missed music for no bird ever sang in his forest now.

"Bravo!" roared the wolf.

The music suddenly stopped.

"Encore!" roared the wolf.
"Rrrrrrrrumpa CRASH!" went the drummer and drum.

"Let's have a fox-trot," growled the wolf.
"Ooooompah pah BANG!" went the big bassoon.

"Who will dance with *me*?" howled the wolf.
"Ting ting CRACK!" went the small triangle and the whole band leapt from the stand.

Rory Wolf felt snubbed and a little peeved.
"What's wrong? I'm not a mangey wolf and I'm certainly not a smelly wolf! Perhaps there's something wrong with them," and Rory Wolf turned to go back to his forest.

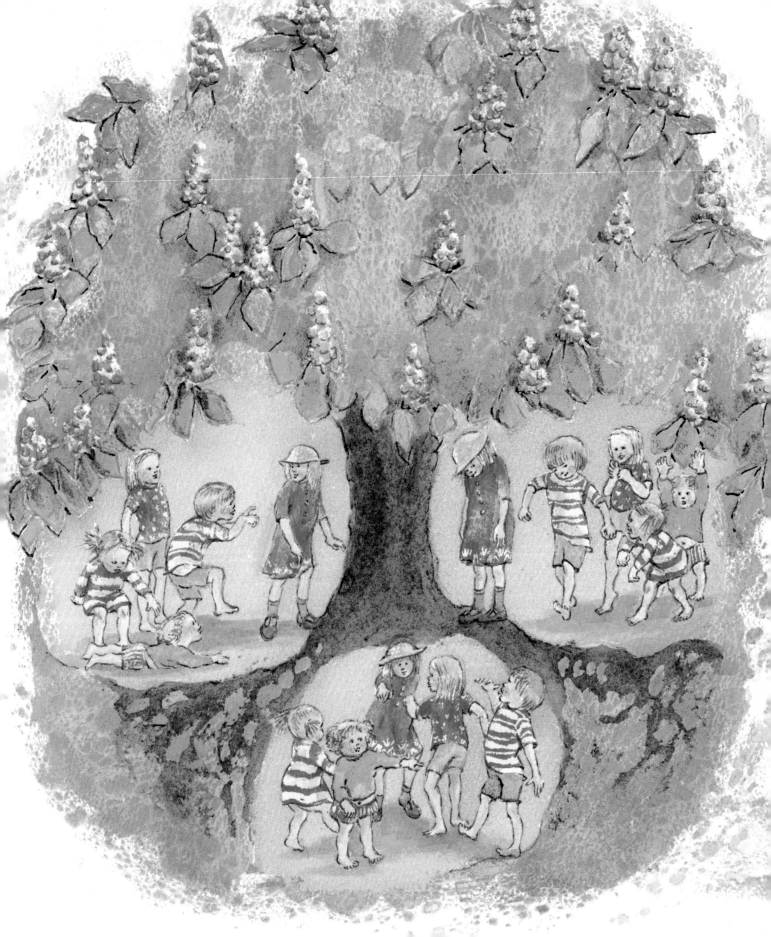

But before he had gone very far he saw some children playing 'What's the time, Mr. Wolf?' That was Rory Wolf's favourite game and he crept up behind them and roared out, "DINNER TIME!"

The children scattered . . .

All, that is, except one girl called Charlotte. She did not mind wolves and just stood and stared at Rory Wolf.

"I only wanted to be friends," puffed the wolf.

"All right," said Charlotte, "But you won't eat me, will you?"

"Do I look as if I would?" asked the wolf with a long and hungry sigh.

So Charlotte and Rory Wolf became friends and played "What's the time Rory Wolf?" and Charlotte was the wolf. But this game made Rory Wolf hungry, so hungry he forgot he was trying to be nice.

"I think it is time to go back to the forest and play 'Who's afraid of the Big Bad Wolf?'", he said, "And it's my turn to be the wolf."

But Charlotte thought she should ask her parents first.

Her mother was frightened. "Don't you ever see that wolf again," she shouted. "Remember the story of Red Riding Hood!"

This made Rory Wolf ashamed; he blamed his mistake on his empty tummy.

Then Charlotte's father got down his gun.

Rory Wolf thought, "I'd better run. I can see this friendship coming to a quick and nasty end!" And he shot off into the night.

Charlotte missed Rory Wolf so much that her father was forced to
buy her a large dog.

"To take her mind off wolves," said her mother.

"To chase the blighters away," said her father.

Charlotte called her dog Rory.

As for Rory Wolf, he missed Charlotte, too, though he carried on his search for a friend, this time climbing high onto the wild windswept mountain. And at last he did find a friend; another wolf like himself. Now Rory Wolf is not lonely any more; he lives in a den on the top of the mountain with his mate and their cub, which Rory Wolf calls Charlotte.